Woof & Quack
in Winter

For new friends and true friends. —J.A.S.

To my parents, Jim & Jean, who let me be myself. —R.S.

Text copyright © 2017
by Jamie A. Swenson
Illustrations copyright © 2017 by Ryan Sias

First Green Light Readers edition 2017

www.hmhco.com
The text of this book is set in ITC Lubalin Graph Std.
The display type is set in ITC Lubalin Graph Std.

Library of Congress Cataloging-in-Publication Data is on file.

ISBN: 978-0-544-95949-1 paper over board
ISBN: 978-0-544-95902-6 paperback

Manufactured in China
SCP 10 9 8 7 6 5 4 3 2 1
4500661230

Green Light Readers

the reader who's ready to GO!

Woof & Quack in Winter

by Jamie A. Swenson
illustrated by Ryan Sias

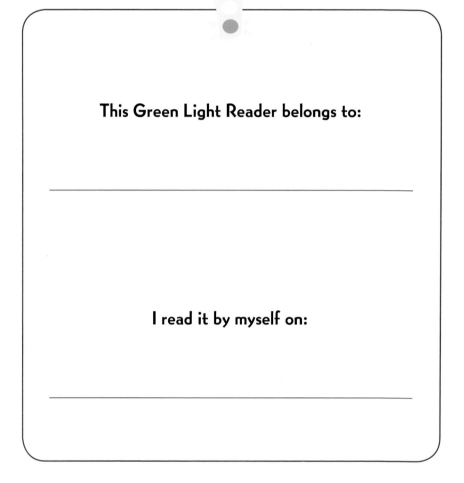

This Green Light Reader belongs to:

_____

I read it by myself on:

_____

Woof & Quack
in Winter

by Jamie A. Swenson

illustrated by Ryan Sias

Houghton Mifflin Harcourt
Boston   New York

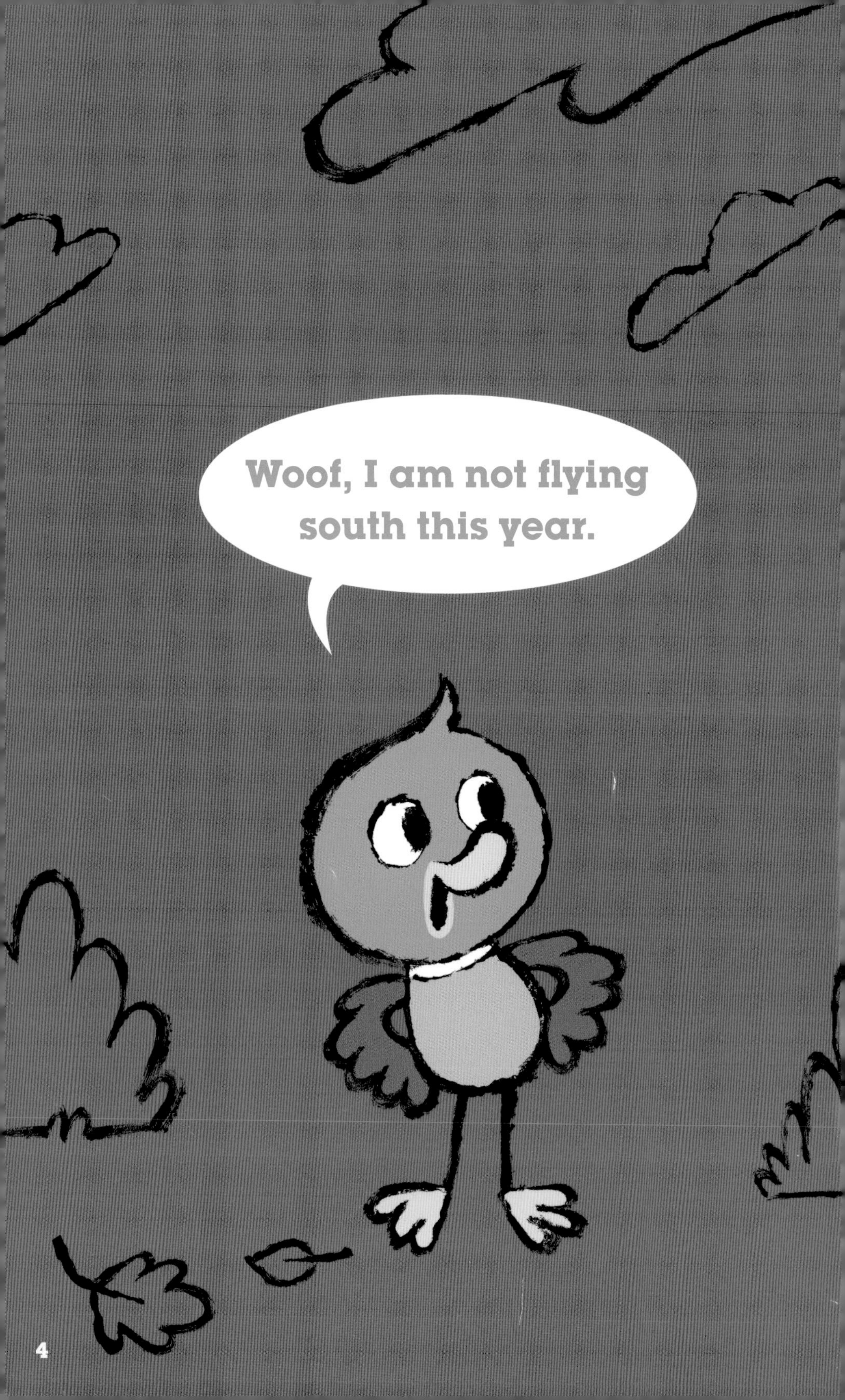
Woof, I am not flying south this year.

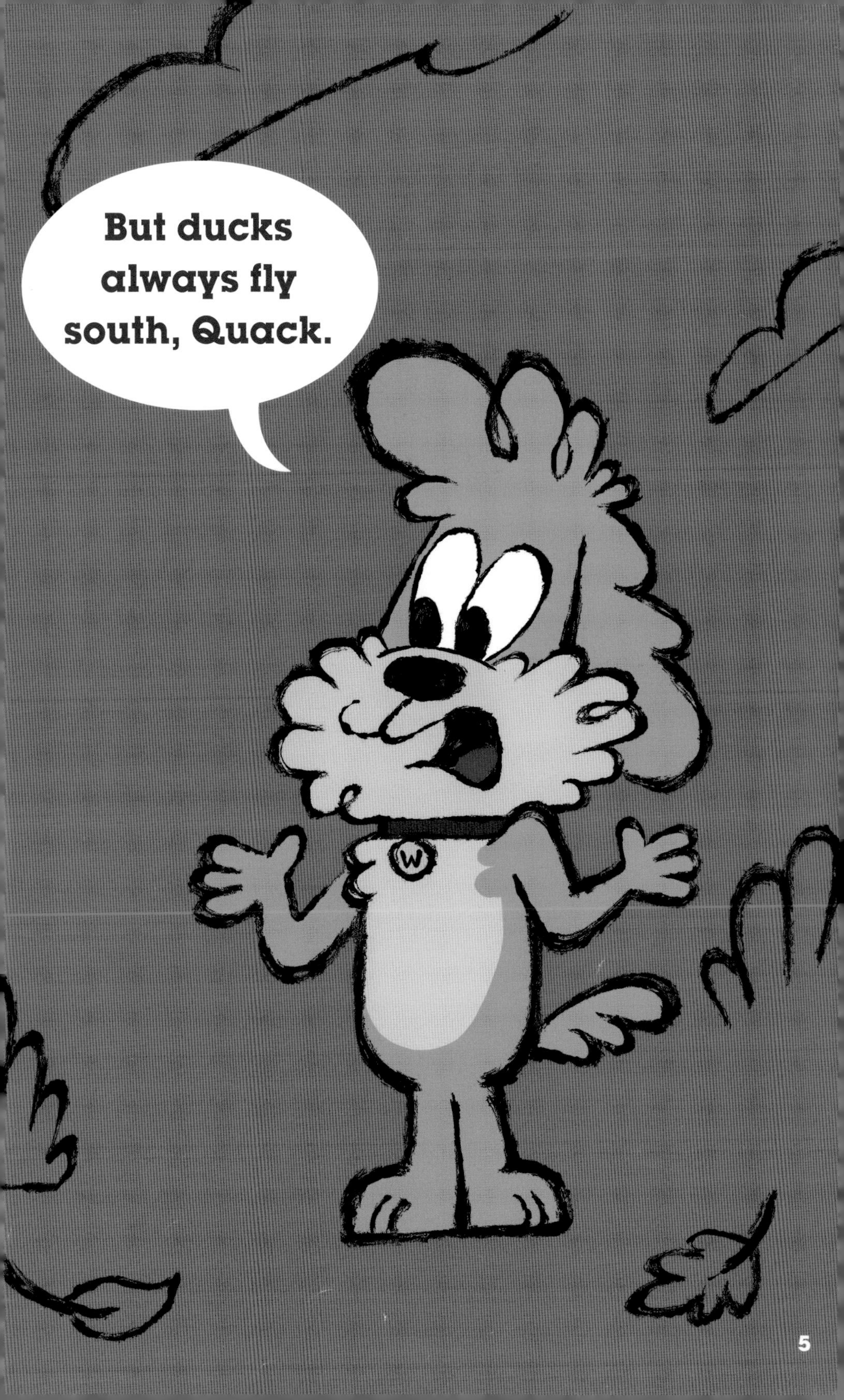
But ducks always fly south, Quack.

I want to stay with you in winter.
This duck is staying put.
It will be too cold for you.
You do not have fur.

7

So Quack did not fly south.
Snow started falling.

Snow covered everything.

Where is the grass?

Under the snow.

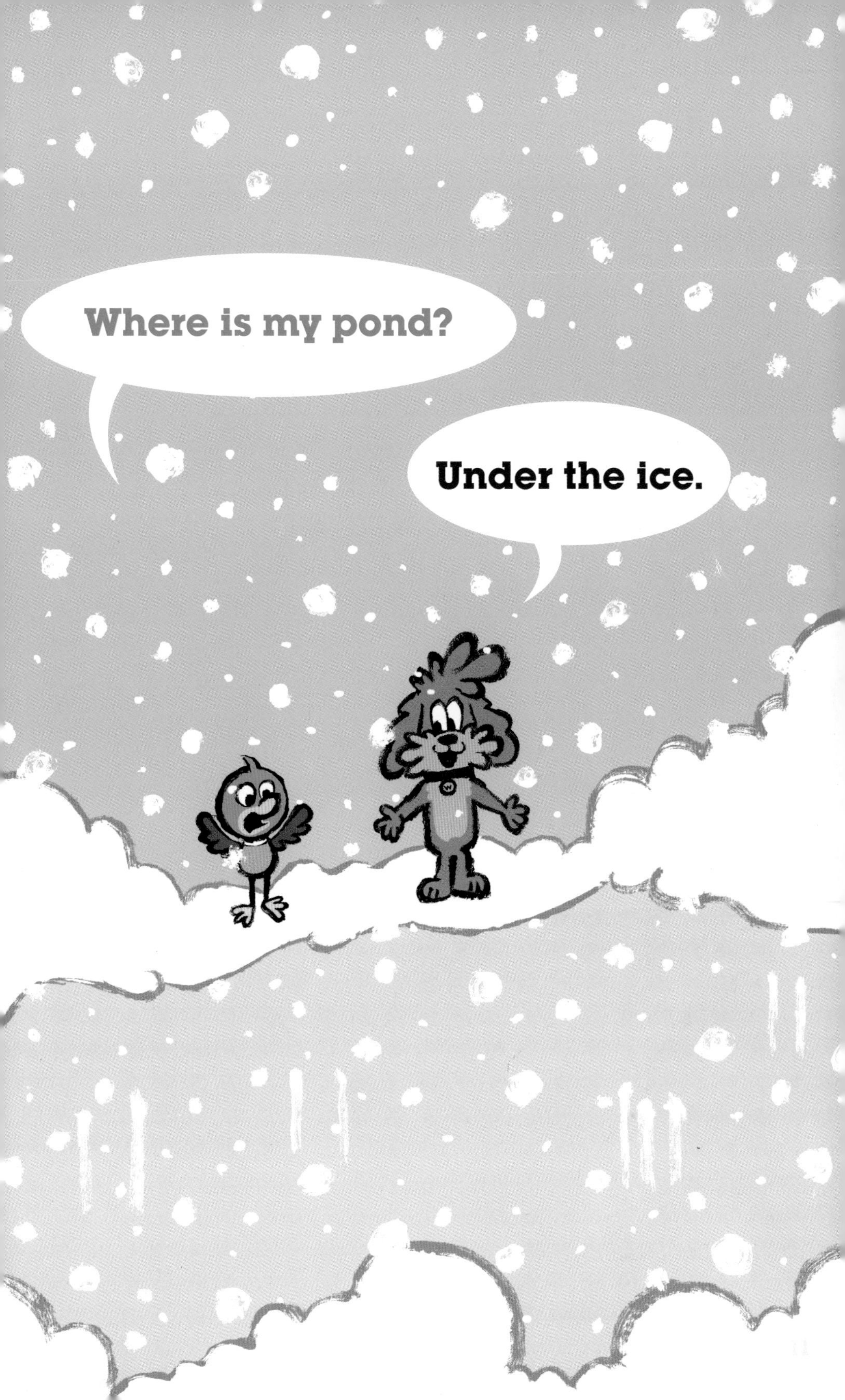
Where is my pond?
Under the ice.

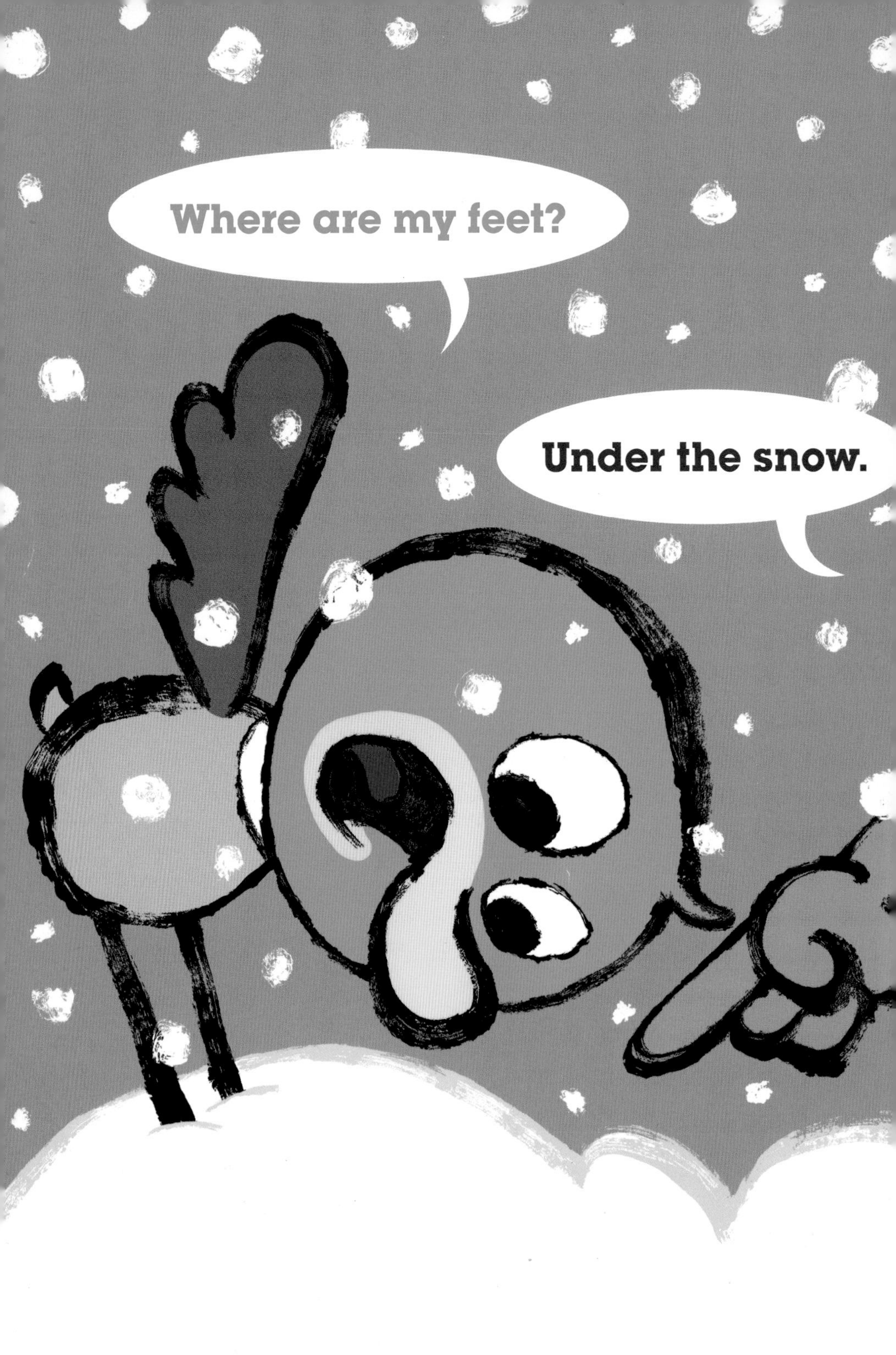
Where are my feet?
Under the snow.

13

Woof and Quack went sledding.

Woof and Quack made a snow duck.

Woof and Quack went ice skating.

BRRrrrrr! Winter is fun. I am glad I stayed put.
I am glad you are here too. But this dog wants to fly south.
SHIVER SHIVER

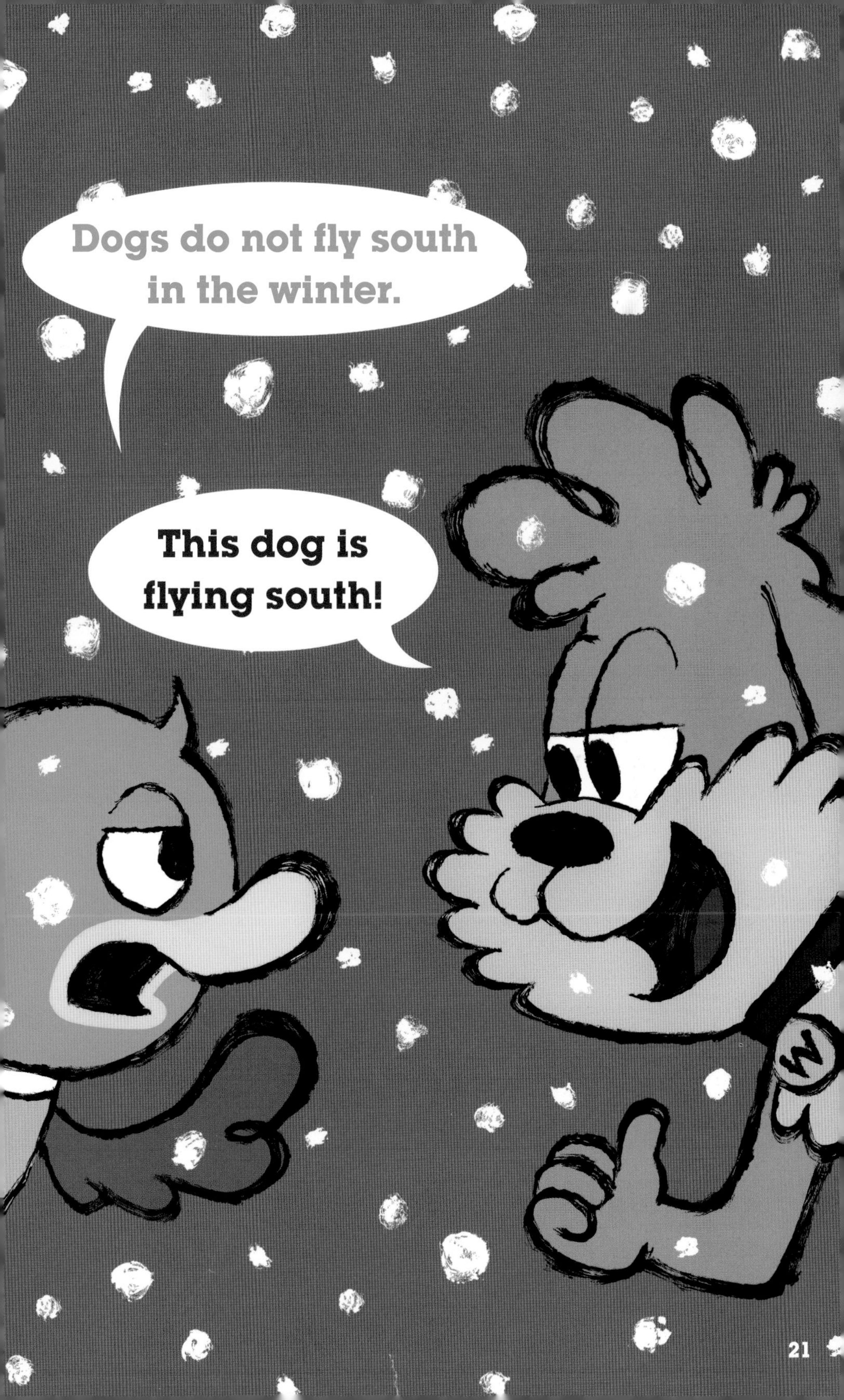
Dogs do not fly south in the winter.
This dog is flying south!

So Woof and Quack flew south.

Woof and Quack went sledding.

Woof and Quack made a sand dog.

Woof and Quack went swimming.